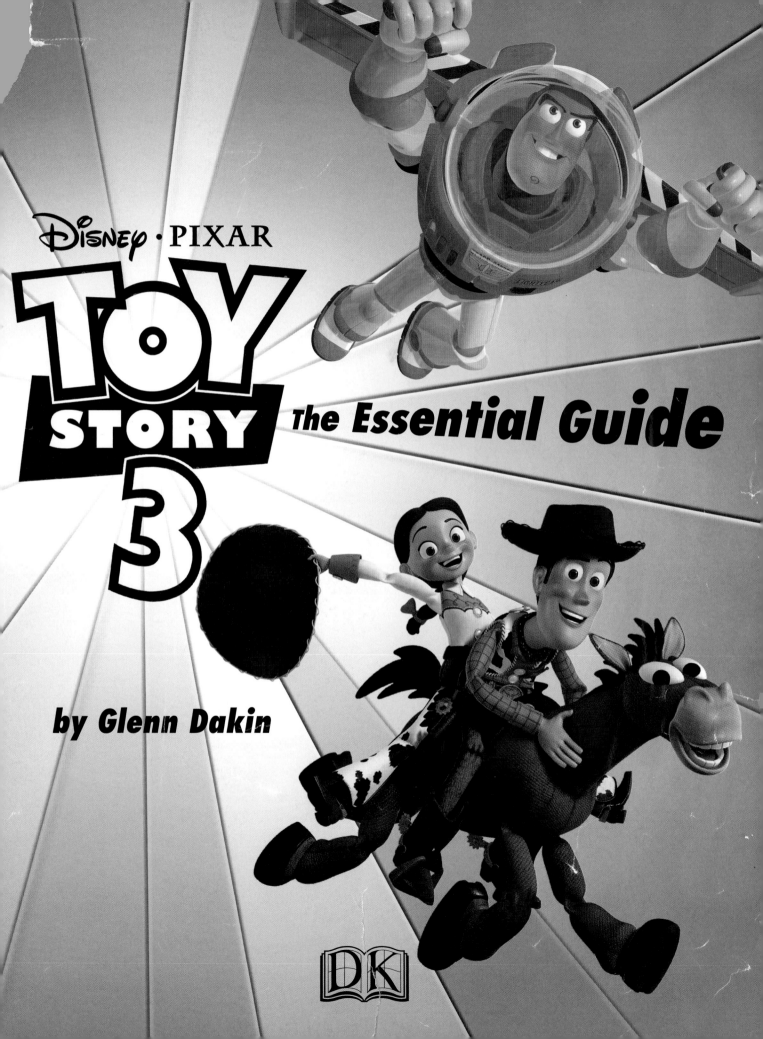

Disney · PIXAR

TOY STORY 3

The Essential Guide

by Glenn Dakin

DK

Buzz Lightyear

This super space ranger is always ready to save the day.

Woody

The sheriff will stay loyal to his owner Andy, no matter what.

Bullseye

Woody's loyal pal, Bullseye, is faster than a speeding train—a toy one, naturally.

Hamm

This perky porker is full of facts, stats, and a little loose change.

Mr. Potato Head

This hot-headed spud is always ready to lend a hand, an eye, or a leg.

Did you know?

Molly loves teen magazines and is crazy about fashion, celebrities, pop music, and all things pink and sparkly.

Molly

Andy's kid sister, Molly, is ten going on sixteen! She's grown out of Barbie dolls, and is constantly plugged into her cell phone, MP3 player, or video games. When she's not reading magazines she's keeping an eye on her brother's bigger bedroom, which she wants for herself.

Molly once loved playing with Andy's toys too, especially Jessie. Mr. Potato Head used to call Molly "Princess Drool" because she was always chewing on him when she was a baby!

Andy's Mom

There are lots of things to sort out before Andy sets off to college. Andy's mom gives him the choice of either storing his toys in the attic or donating them to Sunnyside Daycare to make another child happy. Either way, she needs him to act fast—it's garbage day!

Decision Time

Andy's wagon-wheel toy chest is a relic of the days when he loved everything to do with cowboys. In here are his favorite childhood toys. They are the items that have survived every clear-out and yard sale—until now. They await his attention, forever smiling and eager to play. With a sigh, Andy closes his laptop and opens up this chest of memories, perhaps for the very last time.

"We're Andy's toys!"

Woody

Sheriff Woody is the most loyal toy in the box! He is sure that Andy would never forget his old toys—they've shared too many adventures. However, the other toys don't share Woody's faith and the sheriff is about to face his biggest challenge yet. Will he be able to lead the toys safely to the attic, or will there be a toy rebellion?

Durable vinyl head

Blanket-stitched vest

Voice of Reason

The toys have always looked to calm and confident Woody to be the voice of reason. But what if this time their reliable leader has got it wrong about Andy?

Operation Playtime

When the toys panic that Andy will get rid of them, Woody does his best to reassure them. Unfortunately, this time the gang doesn't want to hear what its leader has to say!

Did you know?

Woody is now a valuable vintage collectible doll, along with his Roundup pals Jessie and Bullseye.

Sheriff Woody is used to rescuing his pals from tricky situations but for once, a rescue attempt by Woody is not greeted with delight.

Best Buddies

They were once rivals, but Buzz and Woody are now the best of pals. However, Woody can't believe that Buzz is ready to say goodbye to Andy. Didn't they promise to stick together to infinity and beyond?

BUZZ LIGHTYEAR

Buzz Lightyear of Star Command is the coolest toy in the universe. If it really is time to say goodbye to Andy, Buzz will need all his space ranger training to keep the family of toys together. This new crisis is going to bring out sides of Buzz's personality even he never knew existed.

Space ranger insignia

Plastic "anti-gravity" boots

Super Hero

Heroic Buzz is no stranger to embarking on dangerous missions. The toy tough guy is always ready to fight the forces of evil and rescue his pals from disaster. But what Buzz doesn't know is that a flick of his switch can turn him from a super hero to a super villain.

Intrepid Buzz shows no fear when he's on a mission. Using a string of yarn as a zipwire, the tentacles of a papier-mâché jellyfish as a swing, and a broom as a pole vault, is just all in a days work for resourceful Buzz!

"We can have a whole new life here, Woody!"

Jessie's Idea

Eagle-eyed Jessie never misses a thing. She is the first to spot the donation box for Sunnyside in Andy's mom's car. This is the toys' ticket to some serious playtime, and Jessie is going to make darn sure no one gets left behind.

Did you know?

After spending years in storage awaiting delivery to a museum, Jessie is terrified of being shut away in the dark again.

Red yarn hair

Authentic rodeo-style shirt

Jessie

Yee haw! This rough-and-tumble cowgirl doll is always first in line when it's time for action. In fact, when Woody's not around, Jessie is happy to step in and lead the posse herself. With Andy about to go to college, Jessie is sadly reminded of how her old owner, Emily, abandoned her. Now she's all set to hit the trail to Sunnyside Daycare.

Woody and Jessie have always been close, but Andy's looming departure has the Roundup toys on opposite sides. Feisty Jessie tells Woody it's time for the toys to be movin' on—just like Andy is.

Bullseye

This trusty toy steed is one of the co-stars of *Woody's Roundup*. Bullseye loves horsing around with Jessie, but he lives for the moment when Woody orders him to "ride like the wind!" Woody can always rely on Bullseye when he needs to make a quick getaway.

Did you know?

Like Woody, Bullseye was famous in the days of black and white TV, with his goofy grin on breakfast bowls, long-playing records, and even a special edition radio.

Machine-stitched seams

Imitation leather saddle

So long, Partner

Back in the good ol' days of *Woody's Roundup*, brave Bullseye and Woody worked together to save the day. But with Andy heading off to college, it might be time for Bullesye and Jessie to say "so long" to Woody.

Forever loyal, Bullseye would follow Woody anywhere. Just the thought of Woody being far away makes Bullseye feel sadder than a lonesome coyote.

Super Steed

Helping Woody save the day is Bullseye's speciality. This heroic horse is always ready to give anyone a ride, especially if they're in peril.

Mr. Potato Head

There's no denying it—this couple really are made for each other. Before his Mrs. came along, Mr. Potato Head used to spend every one of Andy's birthdays hoping and praying that she would be in the pile of presents.

This grouchy spud is a hard-boiled character with a chip on his shoulder. He hates being bossed around, even by Woody. Mr. Potato Head rarely looks on the bright side—well, would *you* if your face kept falling off? But he also entertains the gang with his neat one-line gags.

"We're over the hill!"

Tense Tato

Thick-skinned and sometimes hot-headed, Mr. Potato Head is a rule-breaker—a trait which often lands him in hot water.

All Played Out

Mr. Potato Head has always been picky about who plays with him—after all, it did say "three and up" on his box. Playtime with toddlers leaves him feeling all mashed up!

Mrs. Potato Head

Detachable daisy

Mr. Potato Head's "sweet potato," is her husband's biggest fan. If ever he faces danger, Mrs. Potato Head is always ready to lend him a hand—or any other body part that might come in useful. She's no pushover, though, and is always prepared to give her hubby a good roasting when he steps out of line.

Sweet Potato

Mrs. Potato Head may be hard on the outside but she has a sweet side, too. She adopted three little Alien squeeze-toys after her hubby saved their lives. Now she is devoted to her "boys."

Having detachable body parts has its downside and causes lots of confusion between the spuds. It's not uncommon for Mr. Potato Head to end up wearing Mrs. Potato Head's lips after a toddler play session!

Did you know?
The Potato Heads are hollow and can carry useful spare parts inside them, like angry eyes and kissable lips.

Keeping an Eye Out

Mrs. Potato Head loses an eye when the toys all cram themselves into a storage box. She doesn't know where she lost it, but suddenly she can see visions of somewhere else, and it looks very dusty!

REX

More terrified than terrifying, Rex is one delicate dinosaur. Suffering from a small-roar complex is the least of Rex's worries. He has much bigger things to worry about, like will Andy replace him for a bigger dino toy? Rex can't stand all the uncertainty!

Trio of Toys

Nervous Rex doesn't mind being stuck in the middle of confident Buzz and loyal Slinky. This way, if they run into trouble, he knows he can rely on them to save the day!

"Should we be hysterical?!"

Small claws— big heart

Rex's tail is always knocking things over and he was even given the nickname "Godspilla." But that doesn't mean he enjoys it being snapped off. Being tail-less is just another thing to add to his list of insecurities!

Detachable snap-on tail

Dino Destruction

This soft-hearted dino doesn't realize his own strong points. It's his pointed tail that splits the garbage bag the toys end up in, just like it once saved the day against the evil Zurg.

Did you know?

Rex loves computer games. He once even defeated the evil Emperor Zurg in a video game!

Dr. Porkchop's aircraft

Dr. Porkchop

Cast as the evil Dr. Porkchop in Andy's games, Hamm regularly took on the heroic Woody and Buzz—and lost!

Save My Bacon

It takes a lot to make this proud porker squeal, but being thrown out onto the street finally does the trick. Even Hamm admits it's now time to get hysterical.

HAMM

This classic piggy bank is the shrewdest dude in the toybox. He's a whiz with facts and stats—if there's a manual or map to be read, Hamm doesn't need to be egged on. However, he's liable to hog the limelight when playing the role of evil Dr. Porkchop.

"C'mon. Let's see how much we're going for on eBay."

Did you know?
Hamm has a shy side and doesn't like anyone to see him without his stopper.

Cheerful expression to encourage cash deposits

When it comes to plastic, this piggy knows it all. Hamm points out that attempting to escape from a garbage bag is a waste of time. It's made of triple-ply high-density polyethylene!

Robust plastic exterior

17

slinky

They say a dog is a man's best friend, and that goes for toy dogs and toy men as well. Slinky will go to great lengths to help Woody, and always stands by the sheriff, even when no one else will. He loves taking the role of "force field dog" when it's playtime.

Loyal Dog

When it's time for action, Woody always calls on his faithful hound to stretch the bounds of possibility. Slinky can go places other toys simply can't reach.

"Oh, I've got a kink in my slink!"

Vinyl ears

Wagging metal spring tail

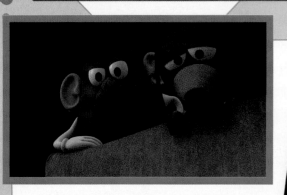

With a dogged determination, Slinky has never let his best pal Woody down. But his loyalty is put to the test when the toys have different ideas about where their future lies.

Modest Mutt

One of Andy's oldest toys, Slinky is a laid back hound with a flexible attitude. He only reveals his talents in an emergency, or when playing the part of One-Eyed Bart's attack dog in Andy's games.

"We are eternally grateful!"

Squishy rubber

*Pizza Planet logo
on space suit*

Aliens

Discovered at *Pizza Planet*, Andy's favorite space-themed restaurant, awaiting the judgement of "the Claw," these squishy, cute Aliens are now in the caring hands of Mr. and Mrs. Potato Head. Old Spudhead once saved their lives and now they are eternally grateful—whether he likes it or not!

The Aliens and the rest of the toys have a lucky escape from an accidental abduction by the garbage man. But taking off without the Potato Heads is not an option for the Aliens!

New World

Ooooh! Surrounded by games and new friends, the Aliens think they have passed through a portal into paradise when they land at Sunnyside. But they are moments away from a serious squishing!

Did you know?

These lovable guys were tied together, hung up, and used as an ornament in a *Pizza Planet* delivery van, before their liberation.

Junk

Andy is the kind of guy who would hang onto his old toys forever, but his mom has put her foot down. It's the attic or the garbage for his toys. Grim faced, the young man grabs a black trash bag…

Dumped!

Some unwanted playthings are sold. Others are donated. But every toy knows that the worst fate of all is the garbage! Andy's toys think they've been well and truly dumped after a terrible garbage bag blunder sees them on a fast track to the landfill. They're crushed by Andy's decision, but that doesn't mean they want to be crushed by the garbage compactor!

The Chosen One

Some old pals simply can't be forgotten. Andy has a special place for Sheriff Woody—and the other toys gasp as the cowboy is tossed into a box of belongings bound for college.

Attic Bound

Andy begins to head up to the attic with his bag of toys. Then, disaster! Molly needs help with her donation box, so Andy leaves the trash bag in the hallway…

Mom swings by and sees the trash bag lying on the floor. She grabs it and takes it out to the curb. Only Woody has spotted the mix-up and only he knows that Andy never planned it this way.

Woody to the Rescue!

Trying to ride into action on Buster backfires—the sheriff is nearly flattened when the flabby old pooch rolls on top of him. Now Woody must act alone.

Uh Oh!

Sliding down the drainpipe, Woody makes it to the front yard—but will he arrive in time to rescue his friends? The garbage man is in headphones, rocking out, and drumming on the recycle bins. He doesn't notice Woody. Time is running out...

Too Late?

Woody can only watch in horror as the garbage truck departs and those last bags are hurled into the crunching compactor! His friends are gone!

Boxing Clever

Woody sighs with relief when he realizes that the toys were all hiding under the recycling bin! Now, thanks to some quick thinking by Jessie, they've found a passport to safety—in Molly's donation box, headed for Sunnyside Daycare. But will Woody be joining them?

Welcome to Sunnyside

With a rainbow over the door and papier-mâché creations hanging in the window, Sunnyside Daycare seems like a haven for donated toys. What more could a toy want than a never-ending stream of children to play with and lots of friendly toys to hang out with? It's enough to fill any play-starved plaything with joy.

Eager eyes, ready for some serious playtime

"Ohhhhhhhh

Enter the Children

This is it! Andy's old toys have been waiting for years to be played with again, and now they're about to meet dozens of laughing, shrieking toddlers. But nothing can prepare them for the mauling they're about to get. Even Molly never treated them like this!

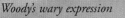
Woody's wary expression

For a moment, Buzz appears to be flying, but alas he's just been thrown across the room by a tiny tearaway!

Caterpillar Room

Welcome to the playroom of the very excitable and very young. Here, Jessie's lovely hair gets used as a paintbrush, Buzz Lightyear makes a handy hammer, and Mr. Potato Head gets a good mashing. The Caterpillar Room toddlers just love to hear the noise a toy makes when they bang it against the wall.

Butterfly Room

When new toys enter the Butterfly Room, they step into a world of imaginative play for older daycare children. Here, dolls get makeovers, teddy bears get cuddles, and toy soldiers fight in safe, pretend wars where nobody gets hurt. However, some selfish toys at Sunnyside want to keep this paradise all to themselves.

Handpainted butterfly decorations

Comfy chair for tired kids and exhausted daycare workers

Slobber-free toys with all their parts intact

Lotso

Lots-o'-Huggin' Bear or Lotso, for short, is a pudgy, smiling teddy who emits the sweet aroma of strawberries. At Sunnyside Daycare, Lotso welcomes newly donated toys, gives them advice on how to survive, and generally seems almost too sweet and kind to be true.

Lotso Hugs

He's a hugger! Lotso is ready to embrace any newcomer who's been yard-saled, second-handed, or just plain thrown out. He tells all new arrivals that no owner means no heartbreak, ever again.

Did you know?

Lotso was once owned by a girl named Daisy. She accidentally left him, and her other favorite toys, behind when she fell asleep at a family picnic! Ever since that day, Lotso hasn't been the same...

Gripping paws for longer-lasting hugs

Lotso's Laws

 Watch out for puddles—always a danger with so many babies and toddlers around!

 New toys must play with the youngest kids—to protect the more senior toys from damage.

Troublemakers spend the night in the sandbox. Lotso won't put up with any rule-breakers.

No toy ever leaves Sunnyside. At least no toy ever has—so far.

"Welcome to Sunnyside, folks!"

Lotso's Promise

Life can be sweet at Sunnyside—if you're one of the lucky ones. Lotso tells Andy's toys they need never worry about growing old. He has spare parts, super glue, and enough batteries to choke a Hungry Hippo.

Disarming smile ....

Twis-Ted

At Sunnyside, toys start at the bottom, pay their dues, and stick to the rules. That way, Lotso stays happy. But if they step out of line, well, they're only hurting themselves.

Soft, cuddly plush with strawberry scent
....

Woody's Round Trip

Time to Vamoose

Woody can't stay at Sunnyside when he knows that Andy still needs him. The other toys are staying put—as Buzz says, their mission with Andy is now complete. It's a sad moment when Woody heads home—alone.

Sunnyside Daycare is a fortress. With a receptionist and janitor minding the place, childproof locks, automatic doors—not to mention the extra guards Lotso has in place—escaping is not an option. But one brave toy makes it out, and then goes right back in again!

Roll With It

A bathroom stall provides the cover for Woody to make his escape. He prefers climbing on the toilet paper to actually touching the toilet. Well, it is best to make a clean getaway!

Hold on to your hats! Woody hangs in there.

Getting out of the bathroom is just the beginning of Woody's problems. The intrepid toy finds himself high above the playground, and freedom is a long way off. Just when he needs inspiration, he spots a handy kite stuck on the roof of Sunnyside.

Bonnie's House

Woody comes down to earth with a bang when a trip on the kite leads him straight into the hands of a sweet, imaginative little girl named Bonnie. Now Woody faces a tea party with a hedgehog, a unicorn, and a triceratops!

Back to Sunnyside

When Bonnie's toys tell the sheriff that Sunnyside is a place of despair and toy torture, he knows he has to save his friends.

Woody stows away in Bonnie's backpack, and is soon back to see the rough treatment his pals are getting.

A grim warning greets Woody on his return. An old toy phone calls to tell the cowboy that there has been a crackdown since he left. Woody should never have come back!

Did you know?

Woody crashes the kite into a tree. Thankfully, his pull-string saves the day when it snags the cowboy on a branch.

Bustin' Out

The toys are thrilled to discover that Woody is still alive, but they tell him that escape is impossible. The cowboy assures them that they will be busting out of Sunnyside that very night!

Jessie tells Woody she was wrong to ignore him and leave Andy. Woody admits he was wrong too, he should never have abandoned his friends.

Barbie

A perky smile, a sing-song voice, and a bright attitude—Barbie can't help being upbeat, she was just made that way! But since Molly dumped her in the donation box, this living doll has proved she's not just a pretty face. Underneath her glamorous exterior, Barbie is as tough as vinyl.

Blue eyes match jumpsuit
....

Image Conscious

Even in the middle of a life-changing crisis, Barbie is perfectly made-up and neatly co-ordinated. Notice the matching hairband, belt, and leg-warmers, plus the cute little bangs. Being dumped is no excuse for letting your image slip.

Barbie is always ready for action in her jumpsuit
....

Sunnyside

Moving On

It's a tough goodbye for Barbie, but not for Molly. Moving into her big brother's room is a chance for her to grow up and shed the embarrassing junk of the past. Playing with dolls is so last year!

Super-stripe leg-warmers
....

Girl Talk

Barbie is sure of a shoulder to cry on when she pours out her troubles to Jessie and Mrs. Potato Head in the donation box. The broken-hearted doll knew that she and Molly were growing apart, but she never dreamed she would get thrown away.

Perfect Match

It's love at first sight when Barbie claps her baby blue eyes on cool, clean-cut Ken at Sunnyside. She's always liked a man who knows how to dress with style, and Ken can even tie an ascot properly. But can he really be as perfect as he looks?

Did you know?

Barbie may look sweet but she is skilled in self-defense. She practices martial arts so that she can wear all the cool outfits and accessories that go with it.

Barbie's Likes:

Pink: Barbie really knows how to work this color. Pink goes with everything!

Good posture: Pose badly and you'll fall over. All dolls know that.

A well-groomed man: Why? Because he'll always have a full-length mirror you can borrow.

Barbie's Dislikes:

Having her affections toyed with.

Bullies: Barbie says that "authority should derive from the consent of the governed. Not from the threat of force!" This doll is deep!

"Totally! Not! Cool!"

Sensible yet stylish hair

Sky-blue ascot

Matching safari-style shorts

Cool blue moccasins

Ken

Mr. Cool and confident, Ken is a handsome carefree guy with impeccable fashion sense. Ken thinks he has it all—until he meets Barbie. Suddenly he is feeling things he's never felt before. Ken's lonely life in the Dream House will never be the same again.

Fashion Victim

Ken can't understand why the other guy toys at Sunnyside don't share his love of fashion. Maybe he's just making the competition too hot for them. If only they would stop calling him a girl's toy!

Ken and Barbie

Ken knows that Barbie is the girl for him from the moment he sets eyes on her stylish leg-warmers. She also tells him something that no toy has ever said to him before—that he's smart! They even share a romantic ride together in Lotso's truck.

Together Forever?

Now they've found each other, it's almost impossible for these sweethearts to say goodbye—ever. Their favorite pastime is saying "I love you," taking it in turns to speak each word. That game just never gets old—at least, not if you're Ken and Barbie! This cute couple has the feeling that they really were made for each other.

Ken's Awesome Outfits

⭐ **Vintage Hawaiian surf trunks**

⭐ **1967 Groovy Formal Collection**

⭐ **Campus Hero college gear with matching sports pennant**

⭐ **Kung-Fu Fighting robes with heroic headband**

⭐ **Mission to Mars space uniform**

Lotso's Man

Living under Lotso's harsh regime has given Ken a dark side. He runs the "Farmer Says" casino inside the Sunnyside vending machine and also conducts the roll call at night, to make sure no toy has escaped! But Ken soon sees the light when he falls for Barbie.

Totally cool New England-style shutters

Awesome saloon-style windows

Painted flowers never need watering—far out!

Cool elevator

Groovy classical porch with twin columns

Ken's Dream House

Check out stylish Ken's deluxe three-story Dream House. Here, Ken lives the dream every day! His cool bachelor pad boasts a disco room complete with a glitter-ball, a walk-in wardrobe, an elevator, and a balcony—perfect for taking in the views of Sunnyside. There's also handy parking for his dune buggy. All that's missing is the perfect girl to share the dream with.

Warm Welcome

When new toys arrive at Sunnyside, Lotso always calls on his right-hand-man, Ken, to wow them with his Dream Tour. Ken's favorite part of the tour is showing off his own Dream House and making the new toys jealous.

Did you know?

Ken's closet room is where the real "magic happens." It contains rails of vintage outfits and a screen to give Ken privacy as he changes into his next fabulous outfit!

Sunnyside's Dark Side

When the merry sound of children's laughter fades away and the janitor switches off the lights, the happy haven of Sunnyside turns into a shadowy, sinister world. Daycare turns into night terrors, and teddy bears make sure life is no picnic.

Gambling Den

Place your bets! This classic "Farmer Says" toy selects random animal noises, making it a perfect toy casino for Lotso's gang. Batteries and play money are accepted as bets by Ken, the creepy croupier.

Placing bets on a "Farmer Says" toy might seem harmless enough but it isn't all fun and games at the den. This is where Lotso's chosen few decide on the fate of new toys—which ones will become "keepers" and which ones are disposable "toddler fodder."

The Mob

They may make fun playmates if you're a kid, but no toy would want to run into this gang of thugs in a dark nursery. Get in their way and they'll take you apart. They've even got a wide selection of instruction manuals to make the job easier.

Expressive eyebrows

Turning Ugly

It doesn't take much to make this bear unbearable. When Mrs. Potato Head mouths off at Lotso, he simply pulls her mouth off. Mr. Potato Head says that no one is allowed to do that—except him!

Did you know?

Lazy Lotso is out of shape because he likes to be driven around in a large truck. He supports his bulky body on a toy walking cane.

Lotso's Henchmen

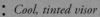

Brains, brawn, and stylish slacks—Lotso's gang has everything it needs to inspire fear and respect. These toys are guaranteed a first-class treatment in the workshop spa, and their pick of the longlife batteries. In return they have to control the daycare's troublemakers. That part has always been easy, so far.

Sparks

Twin caterpillar tracks give this rowdy robot the ability to move quickly over any terrain. Sparks has a playful side and likes to slam-dunk the squeezy Aliens as if they were basketballs.

Stretch

Not quite as friendly as she looks, this stretchy octopus toy is armed and ready to enforce Lotso's laws. Those twisty tentacles are also used for scooping up her play money winnings at Ken's casino.

Tough Toys

Playtime can get pretty rough when Ken and the other henchmen are called into action. Lotso likes to keep his paws clean while they do his dirty work. Removing batteries, rearranging body-parts—these guys will even find your "off" switch if they have to.

Expandable, glittery latex

*Metal-reinforced
attack prod*

Twitch

Proud of his pecs, this battling bug loves to pick a fight. Twitch considers all other toys disposable, even his fellow gang members. He's an expert at needling Ken, especially about his feelings for Barbie.

Pen tattoos

Foul mode

*Fake milk
never goes sour*

*Chubby but
not cuddly*

Chunk

This plastic rock monster is two-faced, but he can't help it, he was built that way. Hit the button on top of Chunk's head and he'll switch from friendly mode to foul. Stone-hearted, he laughs at the sufferings of the new toys.

Big Baby

Meet the real enforcer on Lotso's team. No one argues with this baby, partly because he can't actually talk. Doodled on with ballpoint pen by his owner, and with one broken eye, he lost his innocence young. But babies do learn fast.

Ranger Reboot

Buzz is always full of surprises! Unlike his fellow toys, Buzz is a high-tech item with enough settings to make any toy jealous. But the more complicated something is, the more chances it has to go wrong, as Buzz soon learns after he is caught spying on Lotso's henchmen in the gambling den.

Even space ranger training wouldn't have prepared Buzz for having a sock puppet pulled over his head—by a Big Baby!

Time-Out Terror

In a shadowy closet, Buzz is forced to cool off in the time-out chair. When he refuses to leave his friends and join Lotso's gang, the mean old bear simply gets his crony, the Bookworm, to open the Buzz Lightyear Instruction Manual…

Buzz on Guard

Technical expert Sparks switches Buzz from "play" mode to "demo" mode. Suddenly the Space Ranger's Academy programming comes flooding back to him. Demo mode Buzz is convinced his friends are agents of Zurg so he locks them up!

"Silence, minions of Zurg!"

Spanish Buzz

The locked-up toys stage a prison-riot and take Buzz hostage. With Hamm reading the Buzz Lightyear Instruction Manual, and Rex working the switch, the toys manage to reset Buzz—into Spanish mode! "El Buzzo" soon discovers a flair for dancing, poetry, and picking flowers for Jessie, or "Hessie," his very own "desert flower."

Spanish Buzz is gallant, extravagant, fearless, and a bit of a poseur!

Buzz Vs. El Buzzo

They might look the same but underneath the space suit, Buzz and El Buzzo couldn't be more different. But which one would Jessie prefer?

Straight talker	Smooth talker
Realist	Dreamer
Action man	Gentleman
Practical	Romantic
Two left feet	Light on his feet
Mission leader	Fashion leader

Spanish Buzz wants Jessie and himself to fight Zurg together and to show her the wonders of the galaxy. Even though Jessie can't understand a word El Buzzo is saying, she is charmed by his gentleman ways. Woody just wants the old Buzz back. He's not used to being kissed on both cheeks by a space ranger.

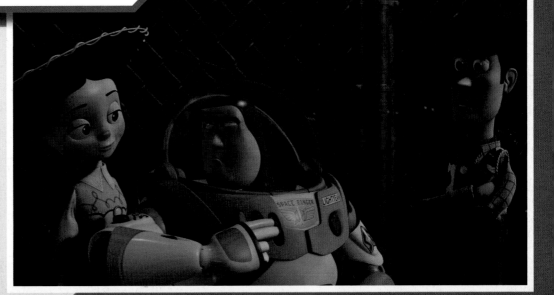

DUMP OF DOOM

Woody finds out that there's only one way out of Sunnyside—the trash chute. The toys hatch an escape plan, but Lotso isn't about to let them get away without a fight. However, it's the furry fraud who takes a ride into the dumpster, thanks to Big Baby. Unfortunately, the evil teddy is not going down alone and his pink paw pulls Woody down with him. Woody's pals are right behind him—after all, no toy gets left behind!

Conveyor of Catastrophe

Andy's toys are soon facing their toughest challenge They thought Sunnyside was a nightmare, but that's play compared to a giant incinerator! Woody and Bu their lives on the line to save Lotso, but the truly evi doesn't return the favor. He leaves the brave toys ru for their lives on a conveyor belt.

Is it the end of the line for the toys?

Long Arm of the Claw

Just when the toys are about to slip into the burning vortex of the trash incinerator, they are pulled to safety by a mysterious force from above. The three squeeze Aliens have taken control of the landfill site's giant crane! Now it's Mr. Potato Head's turn to be eternally grateful.

"Looks like you're all in this together!"

Ready Teddy Go!

Foul furball Lotso gets his comeuppance when a garbage man finds him and straps him to the grille of his truck. A muddy and bug-splattered frog warns Lotso he might want to keep his mouth shut as the truck rumbles forward...

43

Bonnie's Toys

"Are you classically trained?"

At 1225 Sycamore Street, Bonnie lives with her happy crowd of toys. Bonnie's imagination knows no bounds and her playthings do a lot of acting. One minute her toys could be in a café in Paris, the next they could be on a scary adventure in a haunted bakery. Playtime is never dull at Bonnie's house!

Andy's toys are in for a treat!

Nicely groomed plush

Buttercup

Underneath Buttercup's sweet, sparkly exterior he is a gruff, no-nonsense kinda guy. But Buttercup does like to play the odd practical joke and enjoys teasing Woody on his arrival at Bonnie's house.

Permanent glum expression

Squeezable plastic nose

Chuckles

If this colorful circus character looks a little sad, that's because for him life has been anything but a bunch of laughs. Chuckles' first owner Daisy accidentally left all her favorite toys at a roadside rest-stop. Kind Bonnie found a broken Chuckles at Sunnyside and gave him a new home. He's been laughing ever since. Well, on the inside at least!

Giant clown feet

Trixie

This cheerful Triceratops loves playing Bonnie's games. In Trixie's latest role, she has just come back from the doctor with life-changing news! A computer addict, Trixie loves to swap messages with her online friend, VelociSTAR237.

Toothy grin

Neatly cut felt hair

Bright buttons to match bright dress

Beanie-type stuffed body

Dolly

Dolly is a down-to-earth ragdoll, although she sometimes turns into a witch if Bonnie's games take a spooky turn! Dolly isn't crazy about her unoriginal name, and suggests Woody take the chance to improve on his.

"It's showtime!"

Furry prickles are harmless

Mr. Pricklepants

This thespian hedgehog takes his acting very seriously, and he likes to stay in character at all times! Mr. Pricklepants' habit of telling his fellow toys to "Shhh!" has earned him the nickname, Baron von Shush.

Peas-in-a-Pod

Meet Peatey, Peatrice, and Peanelope. This trio of cute plush peas snuggles together in a cozy pea-pod zipper-case. They pop out for a peek at the world when curious, and enjoy some healthy sibling rivalry, which usually ends up with them calling each other "peabrain."

Pea-green felt pod

The New Gang

Stable Mates

Bullseye has really hit the target this time. Instead of being saddled with a hard life at Sunnyside, he's now got a real four-legged friend to be neighborly with—Buttercup!

Meet the coolest crowd of toys you ever saw! When the shrewd sheriff works out a way to get Andy to make a special toy donation to a little girl named Bonnie, he knows he has found the perfect solution for his pals. Finally, the play-starved gang has a new home—and a host of new playmates to hang out with.

Woody is excited to be part of a new gang.

Prehistoric Pals

Rex has always been worried about meeting another dino, but sweet-natured Trixie suits him just fine. Maybe Rex was Trixie's online pal, VelociSTAR237, all along!

LONDON, NEW YORK, MUNICH,
MELBOURNE, and DELHI

Editor Jo Casey
Senior Designer Guy Harvey
Managing Editor Catherine Saunders
Art Director Lisa Lanzarini
Publishing Manager Simon Beecroft
Category Publisher Alex Allan
Production Editor Sean Daly
Print Production Nick Seston

First published in the United States in 2010
by DK Publishing
375 Hudson Street
New York, New York 10014

10 11 12 13 14 10 9 8 7 6 5 4 3 2 1
TD455—05/10

The publisher would like to thank:

Leeann Alameda, Darla K. Anderson, Kelly Bonbright, Magen
Farrar, Cherie Hammond, Jason Katz, Holly Lloyd, Desiree
Mourad, Silvia Palara, Bob Pauley, Brian Tanaka, Dice Tsutsumi,
Lee Unkrich, Jesse Weglein, Clay Welch, Chris Wells, and Timothy
Zohr at Pixar Animation Studios and Chelsea Nissenbaum, Laura
Hitchcock, Shiho Tilley, Lauren Kressel, Tony Fejeran, Leigh Anna
MacFadden, and Scott Tilley at Disney Publishing.

Published in Great Britain by Dorling Kindersley Limited.

DK books are available at special discounts when purchased in bulk for sales
promotions, premiums, fund-raising, or educational use. For details, contact:
DK Publishing Special Markets
375 Hudson Street
New York, New York 10014
SpecialSales@dk.com

A catalog record for this book is available from the Library of Congress.

ISBN: 978-0-7566-6316-2

Color reproduction by Alta Image, UK
Printed and bound at Lake Book Mfg., Inc.

Discover more at
www.dk.com